MIKE YOU

SUPER
AND THE GREEN PLANET

Illustrations by Philip Watkins

G000141642

FREDERICK MULLER LIMITED
LONDON

Sometimes, just sometimes, the planet Earth can settle down to a short time of peace. On these rare occasions SuperTed flies off in his gleaming yellow space station to seek new adventures in outer space.

His video-scanners had some time ago spotted a beautiful green planet, and now was SuperTed's first chance to investigate it.

The green planet was extremely mountainous, but covered with trees and huge fields planted with vegetation which even SuperTed had never seen before.

Soon he was surrounded by cheerful, friendly people who told him that they were called Greenies.

Something about these people puzzled SuperTed. Then he realised what it was. There were no children whatsoever to be seen.

The Greenies seemed worried when SuperTed asked them where all the children were. But they soon trusted the brave bear and told him of the strange invaders from a distant star who had come and stolen all the Greeny children to train them as slaves.

The Greenies were simple, peace-loving people, and the invaders had ordered them to grow food for them and pretend to be happy or they would not see their children again.

The problem was that the Greenies could not give SuperTed any idea as to which part of the planet the invaders had taken the children.

SuperTed decided to investigate alone.

He flew over the land looking for clues. (Can you see any?)

At last he spotted some discoloured patches among the lush, green vegetation. It looked as if the ground had been scorched.

SuperTed could see that the tracks had been made by some sort of machine. He followed the trail of scorched patches until it stopped abruptly.

Looking closely, SuperTed saw that there was a large door in the mountainside. This had been cleverly disguised by allowing a green carpet of leaves and plants to grow up in front of it.

Suddenly the door slid open and two of the invader guards came outside riding on strange walkie-machines. The invaders were very round and fat, with miserable looking faces. One was eating what looked like a large creamy cake, the other was stretching lazily. They both wore belts to which were attached strange sticks dotted with glowing coloured buttons.

SuperTed slipped inside the mountain door without them seeing him.

Inside the mountain a huge underground city had been built. The machine which had made the tracks was parked near a large plastic dome.

SuperTed looked inside and saw lots of Greeny children sitting around looking unhappy.

Suddenly a gruff voice from behind him said, 'Who are you? Where have you come from?' The two guards had come back and surprised SuperTed.

As SuperTed was about to fly at the guards one suddenly pointed one of his strange sticks at him. An electric charge shot out and immediately seemed to send the superbear to sleep.

The guards then made four of the Greeny children carry SuperTed into their prison home.

When SuperTed opened his eyes he found himself surrounded by the Greeny children, who looked very frightened now.

'Don't worry yourselves,' he whispered. 'I realised that the guards had sleep guns. They do not really affect me. I pretended to be put to sleep so that I could speak to you children.'

The children explained that the invaders were the warlike but extremely lazy Tubsies from the planet Flabby.

The smallest Greeny said, 'They have invented machines to do most things but still need slaves to do all the other work on their planet. They are so lazy that they allowed all their growing land to be burned and yellowed by their machines. That is why they needed a new planet on which to grow all their food.'

'Are all the children here?' asked Superted.

'No,' said one of the Greenies. 'Some of them are making Gluto cream — the Tubsies' favourite food — in the food hall.'

'Follow me,' said SuperTed. 'Let's go into action.'

SuperTed burst through the plastic dome wall, followed by the Greenies. The Tubsies on guard immediately pointed their sleep sticks towards SuperTed and pressed the blue, green, red and even the black buttons, making the charges stronger and stronger. But the rays just bounced off SuperTed's chest. He ran towards the guards, who scuttled off on their walkie-machines shouting warnings to the other Tubsies.

SuperTed and the Greenies then rushed to the other Greeny children who were working in the food hall.

Just as they arrived, the Tubsies' leader flew towards them in his blaster-machine. This was so powerful that even SuperTed had to be careful.

He zoomed underneath the machine just as it was about to fire and pointed it upwards.

The machine blasted the whole top off the mountain just like a volcano.

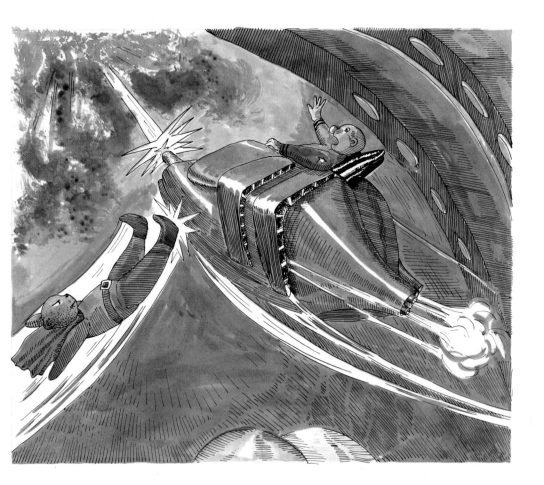

The Greeny children had meanwhile captured the rest of the Tubsies by throwing Gluto cream pies at them, knocking them off their walkie-machines and even causing them to shoot their sleep sticks at each other in fright.

SuperTed returned the children to their parents, and then all the Greeny people were able to live together peacefully again.

As for the Tubsies — well, SuperTed made it his business to ensure that they were too frightened ever to leave their own planet again. They started new lives learning how to look after themselves.

I think they learned their lesson, don't you?